# Wizziwig

## and the
# Weather Machine

## Geraldine McCaughrean

## Illustrated by Wendy Smith

## ORCHARD BOOKS

# WIZZIWIG'S SHED

Meet Wizziwig, the greatest
inventor the world has ever known.
Well, actually, the world does not
know about Wizziwig yet.

But one day she will be famous.
She invents things to make the
world a better place.

Sometimes she lets me help her.
Together we test her new
inventions.

One day I expect we will both be rich and famous.

Not today, but soon.

Last week it was a weather machine.

But there seems to be plenty of weather already, Wizziwig. People are always talking about it. There's weather everyday, almost.

12

13

"But it always comes as a surprise!" cried Wizzi.

"People have to listen to weather forecasts, hope for the best,

carry umbrellas just in case!

Wizziwig's machine had a tank
of hot water, a block of ice,
some rockets and a radio with
lots of knobs.
It had a pair of wind-socks, too.

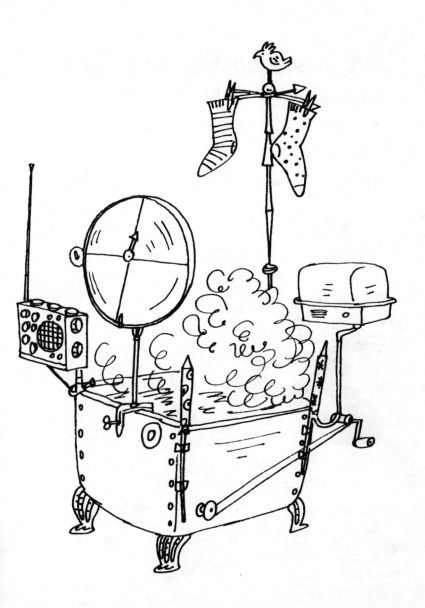

It had a big dial, with pictures.
There was a sun,

a cloud,

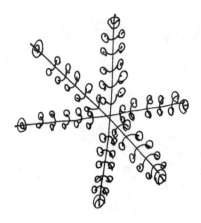

a snowflake.

and a twist of wind

Wizziwig put on her sunglasses.
"I like sunny days

and rainy nights.

I can sit in the garden

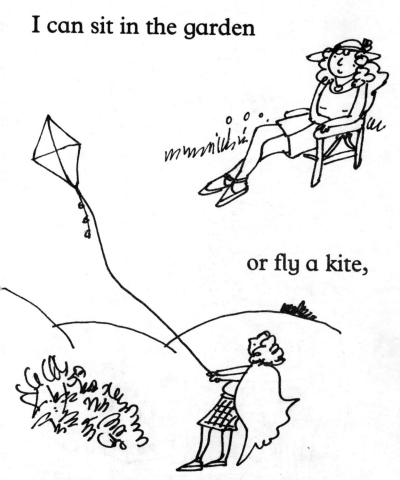

or fly a kite,

But know that the flowers are
quite all right,

She tuned the radio and pressed
the buttons.

The sun came out in
a glory of yellow.
We lazed all day.

Then while we slept,
it rained.

One week later,
a man banged on
the door.
He was angry.

I was busy building
a snowman in
the back garden,
but I could hear
him shouting.

"I make umbrellas! Nobody wants umbrellas when the sun is shining!

Do you want to make me poor?
Turn off your horrible machine!"

Wizziwig shut the door.

Next day
a woman
banged on the
door.
She was angry.

I was sledging
in the back
garden, but I
could hear
her shouting.

"I sell holidays. Nobody wants to go away when the sun is shining!

Do you want to put me out of work?
Turn off your nasty machine!"

Next day
it was a man
from the
TV.

I knew his face,
even when he
was shouting.

"I do the weather forecasts.
Nobody is watching me any more!

They know it will be sunny in the day and rainy at night.

Do you want me to lose my job? Turn off your terrible machine!"

Next day,
a lot of people
came to
the door.
They were angry.

I was skiing
down the roof,
but I could hear
them moaning.

43

"We have nothing to talk about!
The weather is always the same!

Do you want everyone to stop talking?
Turn off your awful machine!"

So Wizziwig turned off her
weather machine and sadly
put back the covers.

"No more sunshine, no more snow,
no more helping the flowers to grow.
No more knowing, the day before,
whether to go out or stay indoors."

The next day,
there was a line
of children
all the way
down the road,
waiting to
visit Wizziwig.

"Can I borrow some rain for my paddling pool?"

"Can I borrow some sun for my birthday party?"

"Can we have some wind for the balloon race?"

Now Wizziwig had never pressed the wind button.

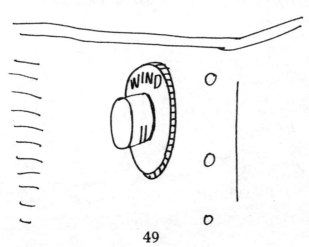

"Do let me press it!" I said.

"Blow wind, and shake the trees;
Billy Buttle wants a breeze.
Dora wants to fly her kite,
so blow, wind, to your heart's
delight!"

The machine juddered and
jumped.

The clouds hurried in front of the
sun and spat rain.

A wind blew in from Russia.

It blew down my snowman.

It blew away my toboggan.

It blew off Wizziwig's roof.

It blew away everyone's umbrellas.

In fact, the wind blew so hard
that the TV station lost its aerial,

and the holiday shop blew into
the next street.

So I turned off the wind.
"There's going to be trouble,
Wizziwig," I said.

Next day, everyone was talking about it.

Next day,
people came
banging at
Wizziwig's door
all day long.

Thank you! Everybody has had to buy new umbrellas!

"Thank you!" laughed the holiday woman. "Everybody wants to leave the country!"

"Thank you!" beamed the weather man. "They have asked me to make a whole programme about odd weather!"

They all gave Wizziwig flowers.
But I am the one who has to
water the flowers.
Wizziwig is too busy.

She is building a new invention.
She is using the bits from the
weather machine.

So I suppose there will be no
more winter sports for me.
Not this summer.

Here are some pages from
Wizziwig's notebook...

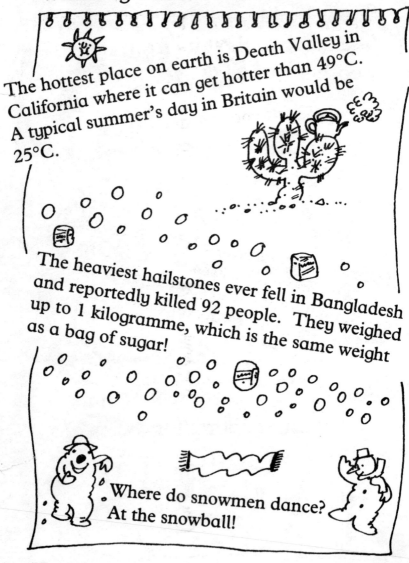

The hottest place on earth is Death Valley in California where it can get hotter than 49°C. A typical summer's day in Britain would be 25°C.

The heaviest hailstones ever fell in Bangladesh and reportedly killed 92 people. They weighed up to 1 kilogramme, which is the same weight as a bag of sugar!

Where do snowmen dance?
At the snowball!

It's raining cats and dogs.
I know, I just stepped in a poodle!

The coldest place on earth is in Antarctica where it can be as cold as -57°C. Apart from birds, only whales and seals can survive because they can escape into the water.

What animal drops from the clouds?
Reindeer!

Here are some other Orchard books you
might like to read...

## A BIRTHDAY FOR BLUEBELL
1 85213 455 0 (hb)   1 85213 456 9 (pb)

## TINY TIM
1 85213 453 4 (hb)   1 85213 454 2 (pb)

## TOO MANY BABIES
1 85213 451 8 (hb)   1 85213 452 6 (pb)

## HOT DOG HARRIS
1 85213 457 7 (hb)   1 85213 458 5 (pb)

## BEETLE AND BUG AND THEIR MAGIC RUG
1 85213 729 0 (hb)   1 85213 804 1 (pb)

## BEETLE AND BUG GO TO TOWN
1 85213 840 8 (hb)   1 85213 879 3 (pb)

## BEETLE AND BUG AT CROAK CASTLE
1 85213 889 0 (hb)   1 86039 008 0 (pb)

## BEETLE AND BUG AND THE PHARAOH'S TOMB
1 85213 890 4 (hb)   1 86039 016 1 (pb)